Enid and the Great Idea

By Cynthia G. Williams
Illustrated by Betty Harper

Published in 2000 by
Broadman & Holman Publishers, Nashville, Tennessee

Printed in the United States of America

ISBN 0-8054-1886-5
Art direction and design by Jennifer Davidson

Scripture quotations are from the *King James Version*.

Library of Congress Cataloging-in-Publication Data

Williams, Cynthia G., 1958-
Enid and the great idea / Cynthia G. Williams ; illustrated by Betty Harper.
p. cm. -- (Our neighborhood)
ISBN 0-8054-1886-5
[1. Pollution--Fiction. 2. City and town life--Fiction. 3. Afro-Americans--Fiction.] I. Harper, Betty, ill. II. Title.

PZ7.W6559235Eq 2000
[E] --dc21

99-047897

1 2 3 4 5 04 03 02 01 00

I dedicate book three to my friend Tam, whose wise counsel renews my heart, mind, and spirit. Thank you for being there for me.

Cynthia G. Williams

And God saw every thing that he had made, and, behold, it was very good.
(Genesis 1:31, KJV)

You're it now!" The joyful laughter coming from Enid and her friends could be heard all over the neighborhood. They were playing kick the can.

"No, I'm not!" shouted Vi. "Ron's it!"

"Oh, no! That one went in the gutter!" Ron saw another empty can and the friends continued the game. Finding cans was easy, cans and trash lined the streets and sidewalks of the neighborhood.

"If I can make it to the end of this corner, then Enid's it again!" yelled Ron.

Ron made it to the corner, so now it was Enid's turn to keep the can moving.

"Got it!" she said.

Enid's feet kept up with the can as it made its way down the street, and then underneath the fence at the neighborhood dump.

Enid stopped in her tracks and peered through the fence.

"Enid, girl, why did you stop?" Vi asked as she ran up to the fence beside her friend.

"The can went under the fence, Vi."

"Well, just find another one," her friend replied.

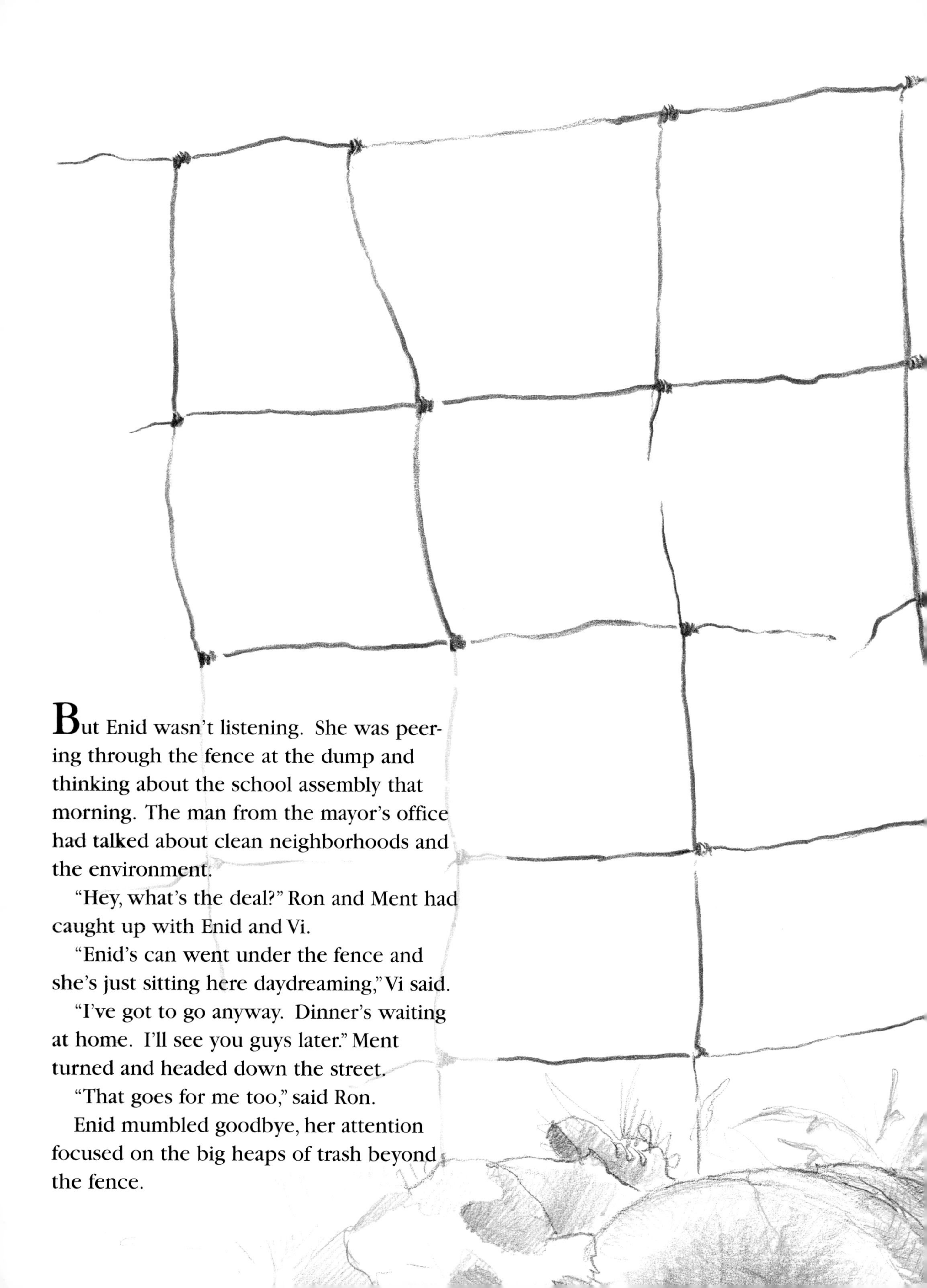

But Enid wasn't listening. She was peering through the fence at the dump and thinking about the school assembly that morning. The man from the mayor's office had talked about clean neighborhoods and the environment.

"Hey, what's the deal?" Ron and Ment had caught up with Enid and Vi.

"Enid's can went under the fence and she's just sitting here daydreaming," Vi said.

"I've got to go anyway. Dinner's waiting at home. I'll see you guys later." Ment turned and headed down the street.

"That goes for me too," said Ron.

Enid mumbled goodbye, her attention focused on the big heaps of trash beyond the fence.

HARPER©

Isn't that your grandma coming from the store?" Vi asked.

"Say, you're right, Vi. I better go help her." Enid called out as she ran to catch up with her grandmother.

"Hello, child," Grandma greeted her. "What have you been doing?"

"Playing kick the can. Can I carry some of those bags, Grandma?"

"Okay, baby, Grandma can always use a little help," she said as she handed Enid the smallest bag. "Did you have a good day at school?"

"It was okay." Enid looked sad.

"Just okay?"

Well, this morning a man came to talk about the bad air and trash on the streets and how we ought to care about keeping our neighborhood clean. After school we were playing down by the dump, and I started thinking about how dirty our neighborhood looks," Enid said looking up at her grandmother. "Why don't people clean up the neighborhood, Grandma?"

Grandma gave a weary smile. "Enid honey, it's because people don't care anymore. 'Don't care don't have no home' my momma used to say."

"What does that mean, Grandma?"

"You see, Enid, anybody can have a house—that's just a roof over your head. A home is how you feel about your house. Anything you love, you take care of, so I guess that's why Momma used to say, 'Don't care don't have no home.'"

AIR
SCHOOL

By the time Enid and Grandma walked home, Enid had made up her mind to do something about her neighborhood. Right after dinner, she ran to her room, changed into her old jeans, and started out the door.

Grandma stopped her.

"Not so fast, young lady. Where do you think you're going?"

"I've got work to do, Grandma. I'll be home before dark."

Enid's grandmother shook her head and went back to stirring the pot of preserves on the stove.

Jemison's
MARKET

It didn't take long for Enid to spot her friends near Mr. Jemison's market. "Hey, you guys, I know a new way we can have lots of fun—"

The sudden sound of Enid's voice startled Vi, and the cans she was stacking toppled over.

"Girl, you scared me half to death, and what are you babbling on about?"

"Enid, you've always got a new project for us," Ron joked.

"No, Ron, this is something really special! Today when the man from the mayor's office talked to us about the environment, and trash, and garbage, and bad air around here and. . ."

"And what?" Vi asked, a little impatient.

"And I thought we could spend a few hours cleaning up our neighborhood."

"Girl, I don't even like cleaning up my room. What makes you think I want to clean up the whole neighborhood?"

"But, Vi, we can do it in no time at all if we do it together. Momma and Grandma will only let me go this far down the street because people have gotten so bad. But if we make the street cleaner, maybe people will change too."

"Enid's got a point." Ment had quit reading to listen.

"I've been noticing how bad our neighborhood looks too, but I never thought about doing something to make it better," said Ron.

MARKET
OPEN
CLOSED
SUNDAY

I can make some signs to put up and remind people to keep it clean around here," Ment said.

"Okay, girl, we're game. Let's get started!" Now Vi was excited. She jumped up and brushed off her hands.

Enid smiled. She knew her friends wouldn't let her down.

"But what are we going to do with the stuff we pick up?" Ron asked.

"We'll put it all in trash bags and throw them in the dumpster by the school!" Enid exclaimed

"But Enid, trash bags cost money," Ron said.

Enid bit her lip and looked down to think.

"Well," she said, reaching into her pocket for her prized tiger-eye marble, "maybe Mr. Jemison will trade us trash bags for some things we have that are important, like my marble."

"I don't think Mr. Jemison's going to take a marble for trash bags," Ment said.

Enid thought for a minute, "I've got a little money saved up from doing chores. Let's put our money together and see if it's enough."

The four friends looked at each other, nodded, grinned, then took off toward home agreeing to meet at Mr. Jemison's store in fifteen minutes.

Mr. Jemison's store always smelled like fresh fruit. Enid and her friends walked up the steps and went inside. Mr. Jemison was sweeping the floor. "And what can I do for you rascals?" he asked.

"Well, we've got this much money," Enid held out her hand full of coins, "and we want to buy some trash bags."

"What do you want trash bags for?" Mr. Jemison leaned on his broom handle and looked from one to another.

"We want to clean up the neighborhood, and we need something to put all the stuff in," Enid said. Her friends nodded.

"Well, that much money won't buy a box of bags, but I'll tell you what—I'll let you have them if all of you promise to come by one afternoon next week and help me around the store."

"It's a deal, Mr. Jemison! It's a deal!" all four shouted. "We promise."

Mr. Jemison gave each of them a box of bags and reminded them to be very careful. With that, Enid and her friends ran out of the store.

MARKET

Enid thought it best if they all stuck together. With their sacks pulled open, they started down the street. Vi and Enid frowned as they stooped to pick up smelly old cans and bottles. Ron and Ment weren't far behind, picking up old newspapers, empty sacks, and candy wrappers.

When Enid stopped for a minute to look down the street, she couldn't help seeing the trash scattered near the new church.

The three friends looked at Enid.

"Don't even think about it!" Ron said, slam-dunking an empty soda can into Vi's sack.

"You know the grownups are having choir practice today, and the last time we bothered them we got in lots of trouble."

"But look at all the trash lying around," Enid said, "and we'll only be there a minute."

Vi, Ron, and Ment knew Enid had made up her mind, and there was no stopping her.

"Okay, but just long enough to get the trash out of the yard," Ment said.

The four could hear the choir practicing as they came closer to the church. Enid bent down to pick up a broken bottle at one side of the building.

"Be careful, girl. Don't cut yourself," Vi said.

Enid looked up to see Ron and Ment peeking inside the church window where the choir was singing.

"Who do you see?" Enid whispered.

"Come look," Ron said softly.

"Hey look, there's Momma!" Enid forgot to whisper. "She's been practicing for a solo on Sunday."

"What are you kids doing here?" came a loud voice.

The children turned to see the church maintenance man, Mr. Moore, with a stern look on his face.

Ment stammered, "We . . . we . . . we're trying to clean up the church yard."

"Well, that's a nice thing to do," Mr. Moore said, "but you're going to disturb the choir."

"We were just looking, and my Momma— " Enid started to say.

"Yeah, but we're finished now," Ment cut her off. "We're outta here."

With that, the four took off down an alley that ran along the side of the church.

They hadn't gone very far before they saw their friend Chester.

Chester always looked forward to seeing the neighborhood kids. Grandma said it was because they reminded him of his grandkids, who lived very far away.

"What's in the bags?" Chester asked.

"Trash and stuff," Enid said.

"What are you kids going to do with a bunch of trash?" asked Chester.

"Well, we're cleaning up the neighborhood to make it look better, then maybe, just maybe, people will start taking better care of it," Enid announced.

"That's a fine project, trying to keep God's beautiful world looking better. But I don't think the four of you should be out here by yourselves."

Enid looked around at the alley. "Want to help us clean up?"

Chester smiled. "Sure, just show me what to do."

Enid gave Chester a trash bag, and the five of them moved down the alley picking up the cans, old tennis shoes, and other junk scattered around.

When they were finished, Chester helped them put what they had collected into the dumpster.

"Thanks for helping, Chester," Enid said with a smile.

"You're welcome. Now y'all run along. It's starting to get late and you should be headed for home."

As they left the alley, Enid glanced back over her shoulder at Chester. He was grinning and shaking his head.

The four passed the neighborhood dump on their way home. They stopped for a few minutes to clean up the ground beside the fence. Soon their bags were full again.

"Girl, I'm tired and I've got to get home," said Vi.

"Me too," Ron said, and Ment nodded.

"Okay, let's throw this last batch away." Enid took a long look up the street. "We made a big difference in just one day."

They were putting the bags in the dumpster when they noticed two men walking toward them. They were carrying some kind of equipment. Enid knew she had seen one of them on TV.

"Boy, are we glad to find you," the reporter said as they came closer to the foursome.

"Are you looking for us?" Ron asked.

"Sure are. When we stopped to get a soda, the grocery store owner told us what you were doing," the reporter said. "We were going to do a story about the neighborhood dump. Say, what are your names?"

The camera man began taping the kids, and one by one they chimed in.

"I'm Vi."

"I'm Ron."

"I'm Ment."

"I'm Enid."

"Whose idea was this cleanup business?" the reporter asked.

Ron, Ment, and Vi all pointed to Enid. The reporter reached down and placed the microphone close to Enid's mouth.

"Well," she started slowly, "in school today we had a program on the environment. When I told Grandma about it she said anything you love you take care of, and then I looked at our neighborhood, the place we call home, and got this idea. Since we all care about our neighborhood and want it to look better, we decided to do something about it."

The reporter smiled and so did Enid's friends.

"Are we gonna be on TV?" Vi wanted to know.

"Yes, tonight," the reporter answered. "But first, we want to get some pictures of you picking up trash."

The four looked around but there wasn't any trash on the ground. Suddenly they all cracked up laughing.

Later that night, there was a news story about the kids cleaning up their neighborhood. In the newscast, the reporter called the four friends "Young Environmentalists."

Enid smiled a big, wide smile as Grandma reached over and gave her a hug. "Thanks to you, it looks like 'Don't Care' has moved out of this neighborhood."

Reflections for Adults

Adults should be good role models for children, but often adults are the ones who learn many lessons from children. In this story, Enid and her neighborhood friends discover that when you care about something you want to take care of it.

As a parent, grandparent, teacher, guardian, or friend, encourage the children in your life to be good caretakers not only of their possessions, but of everything that God has created.

The central theme in *Enid and the Great Idea* is that we must not be careless toward this responsibility.

If you don't know where to begin, look around your neighborhood for opportunities to show others you care. You can make a difference by giving just a few hours of your time.

Thou madest him (man) to have dominion over the works of thy hands. O Lord our Lord, how excellent is thy name in all the earth!
(Psalms 8: 6,9 KJV)